SUPER RABBIT BOY
POWERS UP!

READ MORE PRESS START! BOOKS!

1

2

3

MORE BOOKS COMING SOON!

PRESS START!

SUPER RABBIT BOY POWERS UP!

THOMAS FLINTHAM

BRANCHES™
SCHOLASTIC INC.

FOR ZIGGY

Library of Congress Cataloging-in-Publication Data

Names: Flintham, Thomas, author, illustrator.
Title: Super Rabbit Boy powers up! / by Thomas Flintham.
Description: First edition. | New York, NY : Branches/Scholastic Inc., 2017.
| Series: Press start! | Summary: Tired of always losing to Super Rabbit Boy in their video game world, King Viking goes to the Secret Lands to find the Super Power Up that will give him super powers--Super Rabbit Boy must stop him, but first he must make it past goblins, ghosts, and other video dangers.

ISBN : 978-93-5275-004-7

Subjects: LCSH: Superheroes-Juvenile fiction. | Supervillains-Juvenile fiction. | Video games-Juvenile fiction. | Animals-Juvenile fiction.
| CYAC: Superheroes-Fiction. | Supervillains-Fiction. | Video games-Fiction. | Animals-Fiction.
Classification: LCC PZ7.1.F585 Su 2017 (print) | LCC PZ7.1.F585 (ebook) | DDC [E]--dc23
LC record available at https://lccn.loc.gov/2016042046

First edition, May 2017

This reprint edition March 2024

Printed in India

Edited by Celia Lee
Book design by Baily Crawford

TABLE OF CONTENTS

1 PRESS START! 1

2 THE LEGEND 7

3 THE SECRET LANDS 13

4 THE SECRET DUNGEON 18

5 THE MINI BOSSES 24

6 DOWN BELOW 34

7 DARK SECRETS 44

8 THE POWER OF THREE 52

9 THE LOCKED DOOR 59

10 SUPER POWER! 65

Can I play, too, Sunny?

1 PRESS START!

This is Carrot Castle. It is the home of the bravest hero in all the land: Super Rabbit Boy.

Today, Super Rabbit Boy received a letter. He wondered who it was from.

He opened the strange letter.

DEAR SMELLY RABBIT BOY,

I AM TIRED OF YOU RUINING ALL MY PLANS AND DEFEATING ALL MY ROBOTS. ENOUGH IS ENOUGH!

I AM GOING TO FIND THE LEGENDARY SUPER POWER UP. I WILL USE IT TO BUILD A SUPER POWERFUL AND SUPER UNBEATABLE ROBOT. YOU'LL NEVER BE ABLE TO BEAT ME AGAIN!

I HOPE YOU HAVE A BAD DAY.

YOURS SINCERELY,
KING VIKING

P.S.
YOU SMELL!

Super Rabbit Boy stomped his feet and frowned.

Where is the Super Power Up? Super Rabbit Boy doesn't know. But he does know someone who can help!

2 THE LEGEND

Wisdom Tree is deep inside the Wise Woods. It is the oldest and wisest tree in all of Animal Land.

Super Rabbit Boy tells Wisdom Tree about King Viking's letter and about his plan to use the Super Power Up to build an unbeatable robot.

Flashback . . .

A LONG TIME AGO, THERE LIVED THE POWER PRINCESS. SHE WAS KIND AND VERY MAGICAL. SHE USED HER MAGIC TO CREATE ALL THE POWER UPS IN THE LAND. THE POWER UPS GAVE SPECIAL POWERS TO WHOEVER USED THEM.

ONE DAY, THE PRINCESS CREATED THE SUPER POWER UP. IT WAS MORE POWERFUL THAN ANY POWER UP SHE HAD CREATED.

SHE HID THE SUPER POWER UP IN A SECRET DUNGEON DEEP IN THE SECRET LANDS.

ONLY THE BRAVEST AND SMARTEST HERO WOULD BE ABLE TO FIND IT. BUT NO ONE HAS.

BEFORE THE POWER PRINCESS LEFT ANIMAL LAND, SHE GAVE WISDOM TREE A MAP TO THE SECRET DUNGEON.
P

THE MAP COULD ONLY BE USED IN CASE A HERO REALLY NEEDED THE SUPER POWER UP. WISDOM TREE HAS KEPT IT SAFE FOR ALL THESE YEARS . . .

Back to Super Rabbit Boy and Wisdom Tree . . .

3 THE SECRET LANDS

Super Rabbit Boy sets sail for the Secret Lands in search of the Secret Dungeon.

On the way, Super Rabbit Boy has many mini adventures full of BIG dangers.

Super Rabbit Boy breaks an evil wizard's curse.

He turns a sad prince back into the brave Frog Knight!

Then the Frog Knight helps Super Rabbit Boy defeat a group of gobbling goblins.

Super Rabbit Boy leaves Frog Knight behind. Then he bounces along the Bridge of Boredom.

Next, Super Rabbit Boy climbs Mirror Mountain and beats his evil mirror twin.

Then he enters the Cold, Cold Caves. There, he solves the three riddles of the Riddley Dee.

Finally, he makes his way through the Deep Dark Forest. In the deepest, darkest corner, Super Rabbit Boy finds something!

It's the entrance to the Secret Dungeon!

4 THE SECRET DUNGEON

Super Rabbit Boy enters the dungeon. He sees a large door with three locks on it. Below the large door are three smaller unlocked doors.

Super Rabbit Boy turns and sees a ghost!

Of course! The Super Power Up is behind that big door with three locks. You will need to find the three keys to get inside.
There is one key behind each of those smaller doors. Each key is guarded by a very dangerous mini boss. Beware!

So I need to go through each door and beat all three mini bosses to get the three keys? And those keys will unlock the door to the Super Power Up?
Tee hee! Pretty much.
That sounds easy! Thank you for your help, Plib! Here I go!

5 THE MINI BOSSES

Inside the first door, Super Rabbit Boy finds a dark room full of cobwebs. He sees a key hanging above him.

When Super Rabbit Boy starts walking, he sticks to the webs! The cobwebs really slow him down.

Suddenly, he hears a clicking sound.

It's a giant Spider Boss! She climbs quickly toward him and clicks her pincers!

Super Rabbit Boy runs to the door but he is stuck in the cobwebs. The Spider Boss is getting closer to Super Rabbit Boy!

Just in time, Super Rabbit Boy breaks out of the webs. He speeds through the door!

Super Rabbit Boy goes through the second door. The room is full of heat and bright red fire. He sees the key.

Suddenly, a Flame Boss bursts out of the sea of flames! He throws fireballs at poor Super Rabbit Boy!

Super Rabbit Boy quickly dives back through the door.

The third and final room is really dark. The only light comes from the shining key at the far side of the room.

Super Rabbit Boy steps into the darkness.

Oh no! There's a giant Shadow Boss!

Run, Super Rabbit Boy, run!

6 DOWN BELOW

Super Rabbit Boy makes it out the door and is back in the main room.

He catches his breath.

Plib points to a tunnel. Super Rabbit Boy didn't see that earlier!

The lower levels of the dungeon are full of all kinds of tricks and traps. Bad guys wait around every corner. Super Rabbit Boy needs to find the power ups fast. He hops into action!

Super Rabbit Boy makes it past the bad guys and enters a strange blue room.

There is a glowing blue diamond in the middle of the room.

Super Rabbit Boy can now spray an endless jet of water out of his mouth! It's the perfect power to defeat a fire boss.

Super Rabbit Boy makes his way deeper into the dungeon. He uses his new power to fill a trench with water. He swims across.

Soon, Super Rabbit Boy enters another room. There is a glowing red triangle in the middle of the room.

Super Rabbit Boy can now throw fireballs! It's the perfect power to burn through sticky cobwebs.

Good work, kiddo!
Thanks! I only need one more power up!

Super Rabbit Boy heads even deeper into the dungeon. He uses his new fire and water powers to tackle any creatures he meets.

He looks around for the third power up, but he can't find it.

7 DARK SECRETS

Super Rabbit Boy walks up and down the same places again and again and again.

Maybe there's a hidden switch. May I try?
Sure, go for it.

Super Rabbit Boy starts knocking on every stone in the dungeon.

Let's look online!
Hey! That's cheating!
But we've tried everything!

Super Rabbit Boy stops and looks around. He's been running through the same places, and he feels tired.

He looks at the row of torches in front of him. One light is unlit.

With one tiny fireball, the torch bursts into light.

A secret door opens in the wall!

8 THE POWER OF THREE

Super Rabbit Boy enters a room of pure light. A yellow square circles around him.

Super Rabbit Boy's body is glowing! It's the perfect power to shine in the dark!

Super Rabbit Boy is fully powered up now! He returns to the main room. Plib is waiting.

In the first room, Super Rabbit Boy uses his fire power to burn away the cobwebs.

He scoots past the Spider Boss and grabs the first key!

In the second room, Super Rabbit Boy uses his water power to spray water everywhere!

Soon, all the fires are out and the Flame Boss is defeated!

Super Rabbit Boy grabs the second key.

Super Rabbit Boy steps into the third room. He uses his light power to shine brightly. He's too bright for the Shadow Boss!

Super Rabbit Boy grabs the final key.

9 THE LOCKED DOOR

Super Rabbit Boy uses the three keys to unlock the giant door!

Super Rabbit Boy and Plib go inside. The Super Power Up is waiting.

Oh no! It's King Viking!

King Viking's robot takes the Super Power Up and places it inside its core.

The robot transforms into a Super Unbeatable Robot!

10 SUPER POWER!

Super Rabbit Boy and Plib flee from King Viking.

I am a SUPER MEGA POWER UP! The Power Princess secretly made me just in case there was trouble!
She was one smart princess!
Boing! Boing! Here we go, Plib!
Tee hee!

Plib the Super Mega Power Up transforms Super Rabbit Boy into SUPER MEGA RABBIT BOY!

King Viking's Super Unbeatable Robot swings at Super Mega Rabbit Boy, but nothing happens!

Super Mega Rabbit Boy strikes back with one Super Mega Powered kick!

The Super Unbeatable Robot explodes, which frees the Super Power Up and blasts King Viking through the roof!

Hooray! King Viking and the Super Unbeatable Robot are defeated!

Plib and all the power ups use their powers to blast Super Rabbit Boy all the way home!

THE END.
Hooray!
Thank you for your help, Rue! You can definitely play next time!
We make a great team!

THOMAS FLINTHAM

has always loved to draw and tell stories, and now that is his job! He grew up in Lincoln, England, and studied illustration in Camberwell, London. He now lives by the sea with his wife, Bethany, in Cornwall.

Thomas is the creator of THOMAS FLINTHAM'S BOOK OF MAZES AND PUZZLES and many other books for kids. PRESS START! is his first early chapter book series.

Some things Thomas likes include:

sunny days,

drawing,

walking his dog, Ziggy,

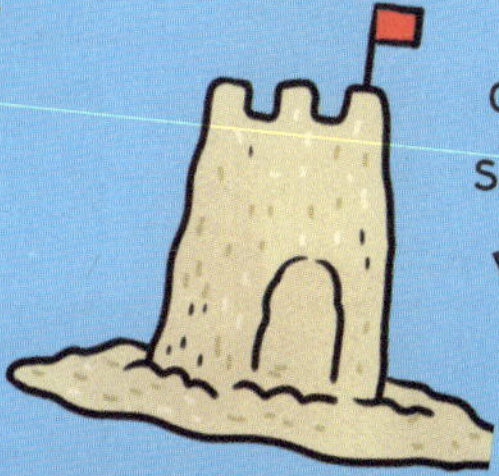

and making sand castles.

PRESS START!

How much do you know about SUPER RABBIT BOY POWERS UP!?

Why doesn't Super Rabbit Boy want King Viking to find the Super Power Up?

What are some of the mini adventures Super Rabbit Boy has on his way to the Secret Dungeon?

How did all three power ups help Super Rabbit Boy defeat the mini bosses behind the doors?

What are some ways Plib helps Super Rabbit Boy throughout the story?

If you could have a power up, which one would you choose? Use words and pictures to explain.

scholastic.com/branches